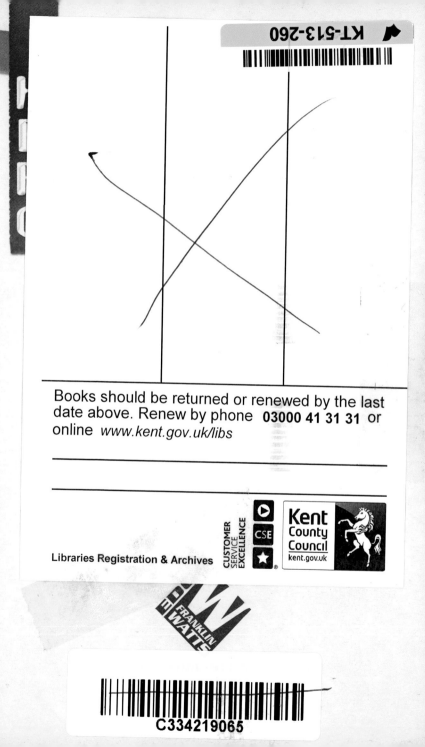

KT-513-260

Books should be returned or renewed by the last
date above. Renew by phone **03000 41 31 31** or
online *www.kent.gov.uk/libs*

FRANKLIN
WATTS

C334219065

Franklin Watts
First published in Great Britain in 2018
by The Watts Publishing Group

Text © Steve Barlow and Steve Skidmore 2018
Illustrations © Andrew Tunney 2018
Cover design: Peter Scoulding
Executive Editor: Adrian Cole

ISBN 978 1 4451 5234 9
ebook ISBN 978 1 4451 5235 6
Library ebook ISBN 978 1 4451 5236 3

1 3 5 7 9 10 8 6 4 2

Printed in Great Britain

Franklin Watts
An imprint of
Hachette Children's Group
Part of The Watts Publishing Group
Carmelite House
50 Victoria Embankment
London EC4Y 0DZ

An Hachette UK Company
www.hachette.co.uk

www.franklinwatts.co.uk

How to be a Legend

Throughout the ages, great men and women have performed deeds so mighty that their names have passed into legend.

Could YOU be one of them?

In this book, you are Athena, the goddess of wisdom and warfare — honoured by the people of ancient Greece. You must make decisions that will affect how the adventure unfolds.

Each section of this book is numbered. At the end of most sections, you will have to make a choice. The choice you make will take you to a different section of the book.

Some of your choices will help you to complete the adventure successfully. But choose carefully, some of your decisions could be fatal!

If you fail, then start the adventure again, and learn from your mistake.

If you choose wisely, you will succeed!

Are you ready to be a hero? Have you got what it takes to become a legend?

You are Athena, goddess of the ancient Greeks and daughter of Zeus, king of the gods. You have left your home on Mount Olympus to help your favourite hero Odysseus escape traps set by Hera, the wife of Zeus. She is powerful, and jealous of your fame. She has the support of Zeus's brother Poseidon, god of the sea, who hates Odysseus.

Even so, despite their plots and schemes, you have brought Odysseus safely back to his home.

You are on Mount Parnassus near the city of Delphi, on your way to visit the Muses, when suddenly you feel sick and dizzy. You are frightened — this has never happened to you before.

As you are wondering what this weakness means, your friend the god Apollo appears.

"I bring grave news," he tells you. "Hera and Poseidon have convinced Zeus that you have defied him by helping Odysseus. Zeus has banished you from Olympus and taken away your powers. You must return to Olympus, and beg Zeus for forgiveness, or you will grow old and die as humans do."

Go to 1.

1

Apollo vanishes before you can ask him any more questions about Hera and Poseidon's plot. Having lost your godly powers, you will have to travel to Olympus on foot, knowing that you can be injured or killed like any mortal woman or man. You have your shield to protect you, and your spear to attack your enemies, but no divine power to defend yourself; and the longer you remain mortal, the more danger you will face on your journey! You consider — should you set out at once, or go to the foot of the mountain and consult the Oracle of Delphi, the wise priestess of Apollo, to find out what your future may hold?

If you wish to head straight for Olympus, go to 12.

If you wish to go to Delphi first, go to 30.

2

You head for the dwelling place of the gods. But as Pegasus flies higher, winged horrors descend from the clouds to attack you. These are the furies. Bat-wings sprout from their

hideous bodies. Their snake-hair hisses around their snarling dog-heads as they wheel around you, their bloodshot eyes burning with rage.

"Beware, rash goddess!" they screech. "Flee our wrath!"

Their claws and teeth rip into both you and Pegasus. You cry out as their brass-studded whips lash your skin.

If you want to fight the furies, go to 29.

If you want to try and reach Olympus another way, go to 31.

If you think you need to seek advice, go to 39.

3

"Fly on!" you tell Pegasus. The winged horse neighs and shakes his head unhappily, but does as he is told.

The moment you enter the storm, the air fills with rain and hail. Pegasus flaps his wings frantically as strong winds buffet him from side to side and cause him to drop suddenly. Flashes of lightning flare brightly in the clouds. Thunder growls all around.

You decide you cannot go on, and try to turn Pegasus to fly out of the storm... A bolt of lightning strikes Pegasus, who screams and rears uncontrollably. You fall from his back and plummet helplessly towards the sea below.

Go to 35.

4

"Great Zeus!" you cry. "Father! I have never done Hera any harm, but her treatment of me has been malicious and unjust. I demand that you punish her!"

The shortness of Zeus's temper is legendary. "Impudent girl!" he roars. "The decision to punish you was mine, not Hera's. Do you question my judgement?"

You realise that you have made a mistake — Hera is Zeus's wife, and he will never take your side against her.

If you want to insist that Zeus punishes Hera, go to 17.

If you feel the time is right to back down, go to 33.

You land in a clearing some way ahead of the centaur hunting party, and wait for them.

After a while, when they fail to appear, you become uneasy. Perhaps the centaurs saw you land, and have decided to hunt you.

Just as you are about to mount Pegasus, an arrow flies from the trees and strikes the winged horse in the shoulder. Pegasus gives a cry and falls to his knees.

Go to 44.

6

You take to your heels and plunge into the forest.

Orion's laughter booms behind you. "Running will not help you, foolish goddess. My companions will hunt you down."

You hear the baying of hounds and the pattering of large paws behind you. Orion's hunting dogs are on your trail!

You burst out of the forest and find yourself between a cliff and a river.

If you wish to climb the cliff, go to14.

If you would rather wade into the river, go to 38.

7

You follow Pegasus up the hillside. The storm rages around you; you are soon soaked, and chilled to the bone.

Pegasus lies down and raises a wing invitingly. You slip underneath it and try to sleep. But the ground is hard, and despite the warmth of Pegasus's feathers you lie awake, wet and shivering.

Just before dawn, you can stand this no longer.

Leaving Pegasus asleep, you make your way down the hillside to try and find shelter. But suddenly, a gigantic figure looms up in front of you. The creature only has one eye. A cyclops! You helped Odysseus escape one of these beasts — they are deadly, and this one has spotted you.

If you want to fight the cyclops, go to 43.
If you want to talk to it, go to 28.

8

You crouch, spear and shield at the ready to meet Poseidon's attack.

But since losing your powers as a goddess you are no match for one of the most powerful gods on Olympus. Poseidon's first strike catches your spear and sends it spinning away. His second smashes your shield to pieces. You are defenceless as he raises his trident to deliver a fatal blow.

Go to 35.

9

You hurl your spear at Orion. It passes straight through his shadowy body and strikes sparks from the rocks of the cliff.

Orion turns and spots you. He roars with laughter. "Foolish goddess. Your mortal weapons cannot harm me!"

He reaches for his bow. His hunting dogs leap towards you, their white teeth gleaming in the moonlight.

Go to 35.

"I hear you!" roars Polyphemus. "I smell you! Who are you?"

You remember how Odysseus tricked the cyclops. "I am nobody," you say.

"You again?" roars Polyphemus. "I'll get you this time!"

The voice of another cyclops echoes from outside. "What are you yelling about, Polyphemus?"

"Nobody, brother!" roars Polyphemus.

"Who've you got in there?"

"Nobody!" shouts Polyphemus.

"Who's hurting you?"

"Nobody!" exclaims Polyphemus, tugging his beard in frustration.

"Shut up then, you loudmouthed lunkhead!"

Polyphemus rushes from the cave. "Who are you calling a lunkhead?"

While the cyclopes are fighting, you sneak out of the cave to find Pegasus and make your escape.

Go to 24.

11

You bring Pegasus in to land in the foothills of Olympus. Asking him to wait until you call, you begin the long, hard climb up the mountain.

Before long, you hear a hissing noise ahead of you. From a gash in the rocks slithers a monstrous snake. This is the python guardian of Olympus.

"Turn back, rasssh goddesss," it hisses. "You shall not passssss."

Wingless dragons emerge from a hundred rocky holes and glide towards you, spitting fire.

If you want to fight the python, go to 49.

If you want to try and reach Olympus another way, go to 31.

If you think you need to seek advice, go to 39.

Night is falling as you set off on your long journey. The sky is clear and the stars are coming out.

You look up as a strange light fills the heavens. You stare in amazement as some of the stars begin to move. The constellation of Orion, the hunter, is dropping from the sky! Bright streaks of falling stars race towards you. They hit the ground with a flash of light and the rumble of thunder.

You are deafened and blinded. When your sight returns, you see a great shadowy figure rise from the ground, blotting out the stars. It is Orion himself, sent back to Earth by Zeus to hunt you down! You hear the baying of hounds as the great hunter nocks an arrow to the string of his bow, and raises it to aim at you!

As Orion shoots his arrow, you duck behind your shield. You feel it quiver as the deadly shaft strikes.

If you have spoken to the Oracle of Delphi, go to 6.

If you have not spoken to the Oracle, go to 23.

13

"Noble centaurs," you say, "I have no quarrel with you, though you have injured my steed. I ask you to heal him."

Some of the centaurs relax a little, but one of them trots forward with his face set in a scowl. "I recognise you," he says. "You are Athena. Three days ago, your friend Hercules wounded our leader Chiron with a poisoned arrow. Chiron now lies dying and in terrible pain. Why should we help you?"

If you wish to help Chiron, go to 40.

If you decide to refuse to help Chiron, go to 48.

14

You climb the cliff, but you have not gone far before Orion's hounds burst from the forest and prowl about, snarling savagely below. Unable to climb, they cannot reach you.

But then a shadow falls across you. Orion himself has arrived. You turn your head to look at him, despair filling you.

"You have escaped my little pets," he says.

"But you cannot escape my arrow!"

He draws back his bowstring. You know you cannot climb quickly enough to escape.

Go to 35.

15

Zeus looks around his great hall. "Athena shall have the chance to put her case. Then we will take a vote. I shall remain neutral. If Hera wins the vote, I shall send Athena away forever, to live and die as a mortal. If Athena wins it, I shall restore her powers and she will take her place among us once again."

Hera and Poseidon look angry at this judgement.

"Gods often interfere in the affairs of men," you say. "Hera and Poseidon tried to destroy Odysseus, I helped him. That is not against our laws."

When you have spoken, Zeus calls for the gods to choose their side. Hermes the messenger; Hades, lord of the Underworld; and Hephaestus, god of fire and forge, stand with Poseidon and Hera. Hestia and Apollo stand by you. They are joined by Artemis the huntress and Aphrodite, goddess of love.

"The vote is five-all," says Zeus. He points at the only god who has not yet voted. "Ares — what do you say?"

The god of war looks around with a sneer. "I have no love for either side. I challenge Athena! If she beats me, I will vote for her."

If you decide to accept his challenge, and fight Ares, go to 42.

If you would rather find another way to win Ares's vote, go to 25.

16

"Zeus sent you here to betray me!" you tell Pegasus. "Go away!"

The winged horse neighs and shakes his head, but you are already running back into the shelter of the trees where Pegasus cannot follow. You hear him take to the air. He flies overhead searching for you, then gives up and flies away.

You are soon lost in the forest. As darkness approaches, you seek shelter in a cave — only for a huge lion to stalk out of it, snarling. It charges towards you. There is only one way to save yourself.

Go to 35.

17

"Yes, I do!" you cry. "You have taken Hera's side against me, though you know she is in the wrong. You are behaving like a tyrant!"

With a bellow of rage, Zeus calls down a thunderbolt. It fizzes and crackles in his hand with raw power. He draws back his arm to cast it straight at you, and send you to oblivion.

Go to 35.

18

"Down!" you order Pegasus.

Obediently, the winged horse glides down towards the island. You see flocks of sheep below as you come in to land.

As soon as Pegasus touches down, the storm breaks; rain pelts down, lightning crackles and thunder growls overhead.

Shielding your eyes with your hand, you spot a cave in the hillside, and quickly make towards it. You call Pegasus to follow, but he shies away from the cave and trots further up the hillside.

If you want to take shelter in the cave, go to 37.

If you decide to follow Pegasus, go to 7.

19

You take the Helm of Darkness, and put it on. You look down and see that your body has become invisible!

Despite your injuries, you set off to climb again, trying to keep as quiet as possible. The python guarding the mountain slithers from its lair — its great snake-head questing from side to side — but you pass the terrible guardian unseen.

After a long, hard climb you pass through the gates of Olympus and make your way to the great square of the city.

Go to 36.

20

You race from your hiding place. Quick as the wind, you snatch up Orion's bow, take an arrow from his quiver and nock it to the string.

Orion's hounds are taken aback for a moment. Then, with savage growls, they tense themselves to leap.

You point the arrow at Orion's heart. "Call them off!" you tell the hunter. "They cannot reach me before this arrow reaches you — and while my weapons may not harm you, I'm sure your own arrows can!"

Orion gestures to the dogs. They back away, and vanish. The hunter raises his face to the sky, and his shadowy body fades away. Looking up, you see that Orion is back in his place among the stars.

Go to 46.

21

You ignore Hera's question, and kneel before Zeus's throne. "Father, if I have offended you, I humbly beg your forgiveness..."

Hera interrupts you. "Do not listen to this lying minx, husband." She turns to her brother, the god of the sea. "Poseidon! Stop this creature's lying mouth forever!"

Snarling with rage, Hera's ally Poseidon steps forward, raising his trident.

If you wish to fight Poseidon, go to 8.
If you want to ask Zeus for help, go to 27.

22

"Bloodthirsty wretches!" you cry. "Why have you injured my steed? Take care how you deal with me, for I am the goddess Athena!"

The centaurs mutter angrily, and their aim does not waver. One of them steps forward. "The gods of Olympus are no longer our friends," he cries. He raises his bow and calls to his followers, "Kill her!"

Go to 35.

23

You raise your spear and cast it at the mighty hunter, aiming for his heart. To your dismay, it passes right through his shadowy body. Orion's mocking laughter fills the sky.

"Stand and fight!" you cry.

Orion's voice is like the sighing of a cold wind through the mountains. "I am a hunter, not a warrior. My hounds will seal your fate."

There is a rustling in the surrounding bushes, and a pack of savage hunting dogs pours into the clearing. These are no phantoms! Without your powers as a goddess, you cannot hope to fight them all. Eyes blazing, jaws wide and teeth shining in the moonlight, they bound forwards to attack you.

Go to 41.

You fly over the sea as the sun rises. Eventually, you see land ahead.

You urge Pegasus to fly lower so you can find out where you are. You see a herd of centaurs. They are carrying bows and seem to be hunting. Centaurs are generally friends to the gods, but they are also wild and hot-tempered.

If you wish to land and speak to the centaurs, go to 5.

If you would rather fly on, go to 34.

You laugh. "Very well, Ares — I accept. Since you have challenged me, I have the choice of weapons. I will set you a riddle — you must answer it correctly to win!"

Ares is furious. "I am a warrior, not a comedian!" he roars. But seeing that the other gods — even those on Hera's side — are laughing at him, he is forced to answer your riddle.

"Answer me this: I leap, I skip, I dance so bright, banishing even the darkest night. Give me food, I fly up high. Give me water and I die. What am I?"

Ares swears and blusters, but he cannot answer the riddle.

"The answer is 'fire'!" you tell him. "And now you must vote for me."

Sulkily, Ares comes to your side.

"I declare Athena the winner," says Zeus, "by six votes to five."

If you want to enjoy your triumph over Hera, go to 47.

If you would rather ask Hera's forgiveness, go to 50.

26

The centaurs have great skills as healers and soon Pegasus is fit to fly again.

But time is pressing. You are growing weaker by the day and know that if you do not reach Olympus soon, it will be too late.

You fly on for a day and a night without stopping. Your human body feels exhausted, but at last you see Mount Olympus rising into the clouds ahead of you.

You are sure Hera and Poseidon will not make it easy for you to reach the home of the gods. You will have to choose your approach carefully.

If you wish to fly to the top of Olympus, go to 2.

If you wish to land and make your way on foot, go to 11.

27

"Great Zeus!" you cry. "You have taken my powers! Protect me from Poseidon."

Zeus stands, and calls down a thunderbolt. He holds this dreadful weapon at the ready.

"Poseidon!" he calls. "I will have no brawling

in this hall!"

Even the god of the sea dare not defy Zeus.
Scowling, Poseidon lowers his weapon.

Zeus's thunderbolt disappears in a blaze of
light.

You kneel before the king of the gods. "All
I ask is the chance to defend myself."

Zeus nods. "Very well."

Go to 15.

28

"Noble cyclops," you cry, "I come in peace."

The cyclops roars and beats his chest. "You are a human! Like the human called Nobody who blinded my brother Polyphemus!"

You remember that Odysseus tricked Polyphemus by calling himself "Nobody".

"I don't know Nobody," you tell the cyclops. "My name is I'm Not."

A voice calls out from one of the caves. "Who are you talking to out there, brother?"

The cyclops replies, "I'm Not."

"Yes, you are. I can hear you!" says the voice. "Who are you talking to?"

"I'm Not!"

"Don't tell me you're not talking when you are, you big bag of wind!"

The cyclops stamps his feet and bellows angrily with rage. "I'll get you for that!" He disappears into the cave, and a furious fight breaks out.

You creep back to the hilltop to find Pegasus and escape.

Go to 24.

29

You urge Pegasus to charge the furies. They dodge him with raucous, mocking cries. You cannot use your spear against such enemies; there are too many of them, and they are too fast. Your shield is no protection from creatures who can attack from several directions at once.

As you and Pegasus weaken, the furies close in, whips cracking, claws tearing and teeth gnashing. In another moment, your mortal life will end!

Go to 35.

30

You stand in front of the priestess of Apollo, Oracle of Delphi.

The priestess does not look at you. Her eyes seem to see far beyond the temple, into other times and other worlds.

"You have a long journey ahead," she says, "and, powerless as you are, you will face many dangers. Yet my Lord Apollo will give you what help he can." She holds up a small pendant — a golden owl with eyes of amber and black opal.

"When in deadly danger, clasp this in your hand. It will bring you back to this place and time."

You thank the priestess and loop the chain of the pendant around your neck, hiding the owl inside your tunic.

Go to 12.

31

You realise that your foes are too deadly and numerous for you to overcome in your powerless state. You break off the unequal contest, and retreat. Your attackers seem content to have driven you back, and do not follow.

You decide to try another way to reach the top of Olympus.

If you made your first attempt on foot, go to 2.

If you made your first attempt by flying, go to 11.

32

"Has Zeus sent you to help me?" you ask. Pegasus neighs and nods his head vigorously. You feel renewed hope. Perhaps Zeus is secretly on your side — or perhaps he thinks you should at least have a chance.

You climb on the horse's back. Moments later, you are in the air heading for Mount Olympus.

As dusk approaches, you are flying over the sea. You look up and see a storm approaching from the north. To reach Olympus you must fly through the storm; but looking down, you spot an island where you might find shelter.

If you want to land on the island, go to 18.
If you would rather fly on into the storm, go to 3.

33

You kneel before the king of the gods. "Great Zeus, I ask your pardon. I do not question your judgement, but I do ask for a chance to defend myself — here, before all the gods of Olympus."

Zeus frowns, but nods. "That is only fair."

Go to 15.

34

You decide to leave the centaurs alone, but your decision comes too late. The hunters have spotted you! There is an outcry. Several of them raise their bows.

Before you can react, a flurry of arrows cuts through the air all around you. One strikes Pegasus in the shoulder. He gives a cry and, wings fluttering, drops to earth in a clumsy landing.

Go to 44.

35

You have no choice but to use the owl pendant given to you by the priestess. You clasp the little bird in your hand.

The scene before you blurs and vanishes. You find yourself back in the Temple of Apollo.

You stand before the sacred altar of the Oracle.

The Priestess of Apollo shakes her head sadly. "You failed to foresee the danger that brought you back here. You must start your journey again — and show better judgement."

Go to 12.

There is only one person in the square — a quiet and motherly goddess who is embroidering a white cloth.

You run towards her joyfully. "Aunt Hestia!"

"Athena." Hestia holds up her work. "I have been following your adventures."

In Hestia's embroidery you see scenes from your journey; your battle with Orion, your adventures with the cyclopes and the centaurs.

Hestia gazes on you with pity and understanding. "It is not easy for a goddess to be a mortal. But the hardest trial is yet to come. You must convince Zeus to set aside his judgement."

She leads you to the great hall, where the gods are gathered, and presents you to Zeus.

Poseidon scowls at you, while Hera glares with hatred in her eyes. "Athena, proud goddess — has your pride been humbled yet?" Hera says.

If you wish to demand that Zeus punishes Hera, go to 4.

If you would rather beg Zeus for mercy, go to 21.

37

"Spend the night in the open, then!" you call after Pegasus. "See if I care!"

You run to the cave. Though you are glad to be out of the rain and safe from the lightning, you quickly notice the stench of decay. A flash of lightning reveals that the cave floor is covered in bones.

You turn to leave this terrible place, but another flash of lightning reveals a gigantic, one-eyed figure in the cave mouth. A cyclops! The creature's single eye is blank and unseeing. This must be Polyphemus, the vicious giant blinded by Odysseus — and you have stumbled into his cave!

If you want to fight your way out of Polyphemus's cave, go to 43.

If you decide to trick the cyclops, go to 10.

38

You wade into the river, as quietly as possible, and follow it back into the forest. The hounds of Orion burst from the trees behind you, just as you reach cover of the undergrowth.

You follow the river back the way you have come, circling round to get behind Orion. You know you cannot escape the hunter; you must defeat him or your fate is sealed.

You raise your spear and creep forward in the cover of the bushes. Orion is standing at the base of the cliff, scanning the rock face. His bow and quiver are propped against the rocks. His dogs are prowling around, panting to continue the chase.

If you want to attack Orion with your spear, go to 9.

If you want to steal Orion's bow, go to 20.

You break away from your enemies, half-fainting from your injuries.

You reach a laurel grove on the lower slopes of Olympus, and kneel in the shade of the trees. "Apollo!" you cry. "I can go no further without your help!"

A faint voice seems to whisper among the leaves. "Look behind you. Under the tree on the left is meat, dipped in the waters of the River Lethe. If the dreaded furies attack you in the air, feed it to them; they will forget their purpose and leave you be.

"Under the tree on the right is the Helmet of Darkness, borrowed from Hades. Wearing it, you may pass your enemies on the ground unseen.

"I can help you no more. Choose your course."

If you want to use the meat, go to 45.

If you want to use the Helm of Darkness, go to 19.

40

"My powers have been taken from me," you tell the centaurs, "but if you guide me to Chiron, I will do what I can."

The centaurs lower their bows. Their leader nods. "Come, then!"

You find Chiron in a forest glade, crying out from pain. You see immediately that there is nothing you can do for him.

You kneel beside the stricken creature. "Father Zeus," you cry, "I cannot heal this noble centaur's wounds. I cannot ease his suffering. Let him die and take his place among the stars!" The centaurs cry out in wonder as Chiron's body fades, then seems to rise from the Earth. As they watch in wonder, a new constellation appears among the stars.

The centaurs bow solemnly to you. "You have helped Chiron to a noble end," says their leader. "We will heal your steed."

Go to 26.

41

"Apollo!" you cry in despair. "Brother! Save me!"

Apollo appears in a halo of light. The hounds are blinded and creep away, whining. Even Orion averts his eyes.

Apollo wraps his cloak around you and carries you through the air. Eventually, he sets your feet back on solid ground.

"You were foolish to set off without seeking advice," Apollo tells you. "I have brought you to the Oracle at Delphi. My priestess will help you." He frowns. "But Zeus will be angry that I saved you from Orion. I will not be able to help you again." He vanishes once more.

Go to 30.

42

"I accept!" you cry.

You raise your shield and lunge at Ares with your spear. But the god of war is crafty, the victor of many battles. He dodges your thrust and brings down his sword to hack the head of your spear from its shaft. A moment later, the deadly blade is at your throat.

Ares laughs. "You have lost, little goddess."

He is right. There is only one escape.

Go to 35.

43

You thrust your spear at the giant's chest, but the point fails to pierce the cyclops's tough hide.

"That tickles!" he roars.

You stab again and again, to no effect. The cyclops lumbers towards you and its giant hands close around you, crushing the breath from your body.

Go to 35.

44

You see at once that Pegasus's wound is serious. He is in no condition to fly.

The centaurs gather around you, arrows ready to shoot. They are clearly upset.

If you want to threaten the centaurs, go to 22.

If you would rather ask for their help, go to 13.

45

You call Pegasus, and together you fly towards the mountain top. The furies pour out of the sky to set upon you, but as you scatter the meat Apollo has left for you, they break off the attack to devour it greedily. Instantly, their bloodshot eyes glaze over, their snarling muzzles slacken into silly doggy grins, and they fly away, bat-wings flapping aimlessly.

You fly on and bring Pegasus in to land in the great square of Olympus.

Go to 36.

A vision of Hera, queen of the gods, appears before you. She does not look pleased.

"You have defeated my first champion," she says coldly. "No doubt you think yourself very clever. But many more dangers lie between you and Olympus. You are doomed, little goddess!"

Hera vanishes before you have time to protest. You pick up your spear and shield, and prepare to set off again on your long, hard journey.

But suddenly, the cliffs echo to the sounds of mighty wingbeats. As dawn breaks, a magnificent flying horse appears against the rising sun to land on the riverbank. You recognise Pegasus and realise he must have been sent by Zeus. But has he been sent to help you? Or to carry you into captivity?

If you wish to approach the horse, go to 32.

If you want to flee from the horse, go to 16.

47

"You have lost, Hera!" you sneer. "Perhaps next time, you will think twice before making false claims against me!"

Hera's anger boils over. "Saucy wretch! Shall the gods share Olympus with such as you? Never!" She signals to Poseidon.

Before you can react, the furious god of the sea snatches you up. You are powerless in his grip as he carries you to the outer wall of Olympus and casts you from the mountain top. You fall screaming towards certain death on the rocks, some three thousand metres below.

Go to 35.

48

"I am not responsible for Hercules's actions," you tell the centaur angrily. "You had no right to shoot my horse in revenge! I will not help you."

"Die, then!" says the centaur, drawing his bow. His followers prepare to shoot.

Pegasus cannot fly and you cannot dodge the centaurs' arrows.

Go to 35.

You raise your spear to menace the python and stand your ground.

But the smaller dragons' fire causes you to dodge and lose your footing on the rough ground. There are far too many for your spear to deal with, and your shield is useless against the crawling horrors.

While you are distracted, the python strikes. You feel its coils around you, crushing the breath from your body.

Go to 35.

You turn to Hera. "If I have offended you, honoured lady, I am sorry."

"Well spoken!" says Zeus. He gestures, and you feel strength return as your powers flood back, and your injuries and weariness vanish.

"You have proved yourself worthy to live among us," says Zeus. "You left Olympus a renegade. You return to it a hero — and a legend!"

LEGENDS

I HERO

KING ARTHUR

STEVE BARLOW ✦ STEVE SKIDMORE
ART BY ANDREW TUNNEY

EDGE

You are Arthur, King of the Britons. Your magical sword Excalibur is a symbol of your power and authority over the land.

Since your reign began, you have gathered together many knights at your castle of Camelot, where you sit with them at the Round Table, ruling the land fairly and fighting against injustice.

However, there are still people in Britain who do not want you as their king. With the Knights of the Round Table, you have fought many successful battles against your enemies, but you know that there are still people plotting against you. You must always be on your guard...

Continue the adventure in:

IHERO LEGENDS
KING ARTHUR

About the 2Steves

"The 2Steves" are
Britain's most popular
writing double act
for young people,
specialising in comedy
and adventure. They

perform regularly in schools and libraries,
and at festivals, taking the power of words
and story to audiences of all ages.

Together they have written many books,
including the *I HERO Immortals* and *iHorror* series.

About the illustrator:
Andrew Tunney (aka 2hands)

Andrew is a freelance artist and writer based in
Manchester, UK. He has worked in illustration, character
design, comics, print, clothing and live-art. His work
has been featured by Comics Alliance, ArtSlant Street,
DigitMag, The Bluecoat, Starburst and Forbidden Planet.
He earned the nickname "2hands" because he can draw
with both hands at once. He is not ambidextrous; he just
works hard.

Also in the I HERO Legends series:

BEOWULF

978 1 4451 5225 7 pb
978 1 4451 5226 4 ebook

FREYA

978 1 4451 5237 0 pb
978 1 4451 5238 7 ebook

HERCULES

978 1 4451 5228 8 pb
978 1 4451 5229 5 ebook

ROBIN HOOD

978 1 4451 5183 0 pb
978 1 4451 5184 7 ebook

Have you read the I HERO Atlantis Quest mini series?

MENACE FROM THE DEEP

978 1 4451 2867 2 pb
978 1 4451 2868 9 ebook

OCEAN ALLIANCE

978 1 4451 2870 2 pb
978 1 4451 2871 9 ebook

BATTLE FOR THE SEAS

978 1 4451 2876 4 pb
978 1 4451 2877 1 ebook

ATLANTIS ASSAULT

978 1 4451 2873 3 pb
978 1 4451 2874 0 ebook

Also by the 2Steves…

978 1 4451 4081 0 pb
978 1 4451 4082 7 eBook

Dragon

Steve Barlow – Steve Skidmore

You are the last Dragon Warrior.
A dark, evil force stirs within the
Iron Mines. Grull the Cruel's
army is on the march! YOU must
stop Grull.

978 1 4451 4088 9 pb
978 1 4451 4087 2 eBook

Mermaid

Steve Barlow – Steve Skidmore

You are a noble mermaid —
your father is King Edmar.
The Tritons are attacking your home
of Coral City. YOU must save the Merrow
people by finding the Lady of the Sea.

978 1 4451 4084 1 pb
978 1 4451 4085 8 eBook

Superhero

Steve Barlow – Steve Skidmore

You are Olympian, a superhero.
Your enemy, Doctor Robotic,
is turning people into mind slaves.
Now YOU must put a stop to his
plans before it's too late!

978 1 4451 3958 6 pb
978 1 4451 3961 6 eBook

Wizard

Steve Barlow – Steve Skidmore

You are a young wizard.
The evil Witch Queen has captured
Prince Bron. Now YOU must rescue
him before she takes control of
Nine Mountain kingdom!